THESEUS AND
THE MINOTAUR

ORPHEUS AND EURYDICE

APOLLO AND DAPHNE

D1369117

THESEUS AND THE MINOTAUR

ORPHEUS AND EURYDICE

APOLLO AND DAPHNE

GERALDINE M^CCAUGHREAN

ILLUSTRATED BY TONY ROSS

ORCHARD BOOKS

For Abigail

ORCHARD BOOKS
96 Leonard Street, London EC2A 4RH
Orchard Books Australia
14 Mars Road, Lane Cove, NSW 2066
ISBN 1 86039 433 7 (hardback)
ISBN 1 86039 529 5 (paperback)
First published in Great Britain 1997
Text © Geraldine McCaughrean 1992
Illustrations © Tony Ross 1997
1 2 3 4 5 6 02 01 00 99 98 97
The right of Geraldine McCaughrean to be identified as the
author and Tony Ross as the illustrator of this
work has been asserted by them in accordance with the
Copyright, Designs and Patents Act, 1988.
A CIP catalogue record for this book is available from the
British Library.
Printed in Great Britain

THESEUS AND THE MINOTAUR

There used to be a great many kings in the world, because every city and island called itself a kingdom. But one king and one island struck fear into all the rest. King Minos of Crete so terrified his neighbours that they paid him tributes every year to be left in peace. It was King Minos who built a palace

with a cellar like a maze. It was King
Minos who kept a monster called the
Minotaur in this famous Labyrinth and
fed it on human flesh.

"Why do we send tributes to Crete
every year?" Prince Theseus asked his
father, the king of Athens.

"To keep King Minos from sinking our ships or making war on us," said King Aegeus (though he did not like to talk about it).

"And what do we send?"

"Seven men and seven women," said the king.

"As slaves?"

"Not as slaves," said the king reluctantly. "To feed the Minotaur."

"How revolting! Never again!" Theseus vowed. "This year I'll go as one of the fourteen, and kill this Minotaur!"

Nothing the king could say would change his mind. As the tribute-ship set sail, the old man called from the dockside, "Good luck, Son! I shall keep watch on the clifftop every day. If you succeed, raise a new white sail. If you fail, raise this black one."

"I shall succeed!" called Theseus.

King Minos laughed to see the prisoners arrive from Athens. "Who'll be first into the Minotaur's den?" he asked.

"I shall," said Theseus, stepping forward. "I, Prince Theseus of Athens, claim that honour!"

"You boasting young puppy,"

snarled Minos. "My Minotaur will make short work of you. Guards! Put the prince into the Labyrinth!"

Behind the throne, the king's plain little daughter, Ariadne, sat listening. She was ashamed of her father's cruelty, and hated to see how he fed the horrible beast in the basement. She was still more unhappy when she saw brave and handsome Theseus dragged away to feed the monster.

Down went Theseus into the dark, but he paused, not knowing which way to go. The guards marched away.

"Prince Theseus!"

It was Ariadne. "Here. Take this."
She dropped down to him a ball of string.
"Even if you can kill the Minotaur, you
won't ever find your way back to the
entrance unless you use this."

"Excellent!" exclaimed Theseus.
"I could marry a girl as clever as you!"
Then he tied one end to the entrance
and went off, unwinding the string as
he went, forgetting everything but
the Minotaur.

But Ariadne
did not forget.

Theseus felt his
way in the dark. It
was true: without the
string he would soon have been
hopelessly lost in the maze of winding
corridors. Suddenly, his fingers brushed
warm, wiry hair, then the bony curve of
a horn. The Minotaur bellowed in his
ear and flung him through the darkness.

It stamped on him with sharp hoofs.
The string was knocked out of his hand.

They fought in utter darkness. The
monster, half-man, half-bull, crushed
him between hairy arms and lashed him
with its tail. But Theseus took hold of
the horns and twisted them first one

way, then the other. He kicked and
butted and struggled, and at last the
beast gave a gurgling gasp and fell dead.

Filled with panic, the prince
scrabbled around for the ball of string.
There! No, that was the Minotaur's ear.
There! Yes! Now he had only to wind it

in and so retrace his steps.

At the door of the Labyrinth, Ariadne stood waiting.

"You're alive! You escaped!" she cried, and she took him by the hand and hurried him away.

They freed the other thirteen prisoners, then ran to the harbour. "You must take me with you, or my father will kill me too!" said the princess.

"Of course! Come aboard!" said

Theseus, raising the old black sail with two pulls of his strong arms. The sail filled, and they were at sea before anyone knew they had escaped.

Theseus sat on deck in the sunshine and thought about what he had done. He was proud. His father would be proud, too. "I must change this sail for a white one," he was thinking.

Just then, Ariadne came and sat at his feet, gazing up at him. "How wonderful!" she sighed. "To be free of my wicked father and to be married to a brave prince!"

"Married?" said Theseus, turning rather pale. He suddenly realised that just because Ariadne had saved his life,

she expected to marry him! He studied
her face. That nose was very big. And
those eyebrows were very thick.
"Mmmm," he said. "How wonderful."

On the way home, the ship put in at
an island for supplies. Theseus sent
Ariadne ashore to buy wine and bread.
While she was gone, he set sail and
hurried away, breathing a sigh of relief.

"When I marry," he thought, "it will be to a beautiful queen or a goddess." He was in such a hurry to get away that he quite forgot to change the black sail for a white one.

King Aegeus, watching day after day from the cliff below Athens, saw the ship as it hove into view. He saw the black sail full of wind. And in that moment, he believed that his son Theseus had been killed and eaten by the Minotaur. He threw himself off the high white cliff into the water below.

And ever afterwards the sea was called the Aegean Sea, after the father of that ungrateful hero, Theseus.

ORPHEUS AND EURYDICE

There were once a man and wife so much in love that they wanted nothing but each other. Her name was Eurydice and his was Orpheus. Orpheus was a musician.

Oh, and what a musician! He played a lyre and he sang such songs that the grass at his feet curled with pleasure. Snarling wild animals purred and waved their tails. The trees swayed towards him, tilting their leaves like ears.

Then one day a snake stung Eurydice. She gave a cry of pain and fell to her knees. Orpheus caught her in his arms. "Eurydice! What's the matter!" he cried.

But she could not answer. She was dead. Orpheus was left holding her body, but her soul slipped out of his grasp and sank into the dry, cracked ground—down into the Underworld.

Then Orpheus stopped singing and laid down his lyre. "There is no life without Eurydice," he said. "I must fetch her back."

His friends gasped with horror at such an idea. But Orpheus turned his back on them and travelled down, through the valleys, pits and tunnels of the world, to the shores of the River Styx.

At the river bank Orpheus called out, "Ferryman! Ferryman! Come and row me over, for my wife has come to the Underworld too early, and I must fetch her back home."

There was a splash of oars and a black boat appeared out of the mists.

"Young man, are you mad? No one but the Dead may cross this river and enter the Underworld! Even if I did row you over, you couldn't get past Cerberus who guards the gate!"

"I must," said Orpheus, and the ferryman was so struck by the grief in the young man's face that he let him step aboard.

As the boat glided across the river, a dark shape loomed up, then a terrible barking split the air. It was Cerberus, the three-headed guard dog. Orpheus took his lyre on to his lap and began to play. He played a song without words, and the ferryman stopped splashing his oars to listen. The barking sank to a

yelp, then to a whimper. When the boat
touched shore, Orpheus stepped out of
the boat, still playing.

Throughout the Underworld, the
souls of the Dead stopped to listen.
Pluto, King of the Dead, also listened.
"What's that noise, wife?"

His wife, Persephone, knew at once.
"It must be Orpheus the musician! Oh,
if he is dead and his spirit ours to keep,
we shall have better music here than
on earth!"

"Never! Music is forbidden here!" exclaimed Pluto.

At the sight of Orpheus—a man still wearing his earthly body—Pluto jumped up and pointed an angry finger. "You'll be sorry you dared to sneak down here, young man!"

Orpheus simply began to sing. He sang of Eurydice's beauty. He sang of their love. He sang of the spiteful snake and of his unbearable loneliness. When the song finished, Pluto sank back in his throne, his hands over his face, and tears running down into his beard.

"Every time someone dies, there are people who want them alive again," said Pluto. "But you are the only one who ever made me allow this to happen. Eurydice shall return to the earth."

He clapped his hands, and feet could be heard running down a long corridor: the footsteps of Eurydice. Orpheus peered through the gloom for a first glimpse of her dear face.

"If—" said Pluto.

"If?"

"If you can climb back into the sunlight without once turning to look at her face." He laughed unkindly.

Back Orpheus went towards the River Styx, and the swish of a woman's robes followed him. But he did not look back. Again Orpheus began to play.

Again the great dog Cerberus lolled
with delight and let him pass, licking
him with three tongues. But Orpheus
did not look back. Into the rowing boat
he stepped, and someone stepped in
behind him. The ferryman rowed two
passengers across the river.

One last long climb and they would
be free of the Underworld! Then
Orpheus would be able to take

Eurydice in his arms and kiss her and laugh about the dreary Kingdom of the Dead. "Not long now!" he called to her.

Why did Eurydice not reply? Perhaps Pluto had tricked him. Perhaps it was someone else following him. Or perhaps Eurydice had changed during her time in the Underworld, and didn't love her husband any more! Just as the first rays of sunlight came into view,

Orpheus glanced quickly over his shoulder—just to be sure.

Oh yes, it was Eurydice. Those eyes, that hair, that sweet mouth calling his name: "Orpheus!"

She sank down like a drowning swimmer: "Orpheus, why?" she fell back down and the darkness swallowed her up.

"Eurydice!"

But she was gone. Orpheus had lost his beloved a second time.

Orpheus was so broken-hearted that he could never again play cheerful music. When he touched his lyre, the notes sobbed out of it like tears.

"Play us something jolly, can't you?" demanded his audiences. But Orpheus played the only music he could. "Something jolly, we said!" And when he would not, they attacked him —and finally killed him.

His soul rushed out of his body, eager to reach the gloomy Underworld. "Let me go down to Eurydice!" he cried. "Surely I can, now that I'm dead?"

But the gods replied, "You shan't go down to the Underworld, Orpheus. Your music has given us such pleasure that your lyre shall be turned into stars and hung up in the night sky."

"But..." began Orpheus.

"And you shall live out eternity in that special place reserved for those loved by the gods. And Eurydice shall live there with you."

So the two spirits floated hand in hand to the Fields of Eternal happiness, to sing and make music together for ever.

APOLLO AND DAPHNE

There was one god who was younger than all the others. Cupid was no more than a boy, but for all that, he was trusted to look after the most important thing of all; falling in love. With his bow and arrows he could shoot straight into the heart of any man or woman. And once his arrow struck, there was no cure for the wound.

One day, when Apollo the sun god saw Cupid with his tiny bow and arrow, he laughed rudely and said. "What's a baby doing carrying the weapons of a warrior? You should leave archery to grown-ups like me!"

Cupid was so angry that he took a gold-tipped arrow from his quiver and shot it, point blank, into Apollo's chest. The sun god felt no pain—well, only a pang. "Ha! Is that the best you can do?" he jeered at Cupid.

Apollo thought he knew all about love.

Women were always falling in love with him because he was so handsome. But only when Cupid's golden arrow pierced him did he find out how it felt to be in love himself. His eye came to rest on Daphne—a water nymph, daughter of the River Peleus. And all at once she was Daphne his passion, his dearest darling, his one desire.

Then Cupid fired a second arrow—tipped this time with lead. It pierced Daphne's breast and filled her heart—not with love—but with loathing. From that moment, she hated all men.

"Daphne, I love you!" declared Apollo but Daphne took to her heels and ran. Through the woods she ran,

across the meadows and mountains.

"Come back, Daphne! Where are you going? Why are you running away? I love you! I only want to kiss you and hold you close and tell you how much I love you!"

"Leave me alone!" cried Daphne. "I don't want your love! I don't want your kisses! Stop following me!"

She was fast, but Apollo was faster. He began to catch up with her, so that when he reached out he could feel her hair brush the tips of his fingers. "Don't be afraid! I wouldn't hurt you, would I, loving you the way I do?" The harder she ran, the more he wanted to catch her.

Down ran Daphne to the brink of the river. "Oh, Father River! Help me, please! He has hold of me by my hair! Save me! Save me from Apollo!"

When the river saw how afraid she was, he took pity on her.

"Got you!" cried Apollo triumphantly, catching hold of both her arms.

But suddenly his hands were full of splinters. Ahead of him, Daphne stopped so suddenly that he bloodied his nose and scraped his shins against bark. For Daphne's brown feet had slipped into the soil and taken root, and her arms had turned to branches and her tears to falling leaves. The river had turned her into a green bay tree, and there she stood, trembling, but only because of the breeze.

"I wanted you for my own!" cried Apollo. "If I can't have you as a woman, I'll have you as you are. From today onwards, I declare that the bay tree is sacred to me, the god Apollo. Let every victorious hero returning from the wars, every emperor and king be crowned with a wreath of bay leaves, because Apollo's first love was the green bay tree."

Then he brushed the leaves out of his hair and looked about him for a more friendly woman—one who would smile at him rather than run away.